Bob the Builder™

Scoop's Stegosaurus

It was a busy morning at the yard. Bob, Scoop and Lofty were off to Farmer Pickles's farm to lay some new pipes. Wendy was going into town to build some cabinets for the museum.

"Oh Wendy, I've never seen a museum," squeaked Dizzy. "Can I come too, pleeeasse?"

Wendy smiled at Dizzy. "I don't see why not," she said.

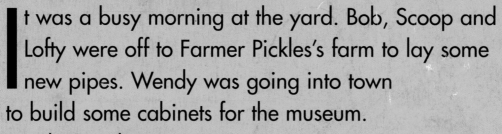

2

"Yesss!" Dizzy said, spinning round and round. "Thanks, Wendy!"

"Right then, team," said Bob, "off to work!"

"**Can we fix it?**" called Scoop.

"**Yes, we can!**" everyone answered.

"Er, yeah… I think so," said Lofty as they left the yard.

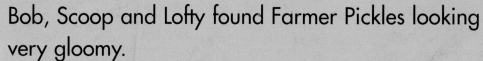

Bob, Scoop and Lofty found Farmer Pickles looking very gloomy.

"All this rain we've been having has made my field so muddy nothing will grow in it," he said, picking up a droopy wet plant.

"Don't worry Farmer Pickles, these pipes will drain the water off the field in no time," said Bob cheerfully.

In the museum Wendy was busy measuring the display cabinets.

Dizzy was talking to Mr Ellis, the museum curator.

"See this," he said, holding up a pot.

"It's all old and cracked," said Dizzy.

"That's because it's over four thousand years old," Mr Ellis replied. "And that means that people have been living around here for ages!"

"Wow!" gasped Dizzy in amazement.

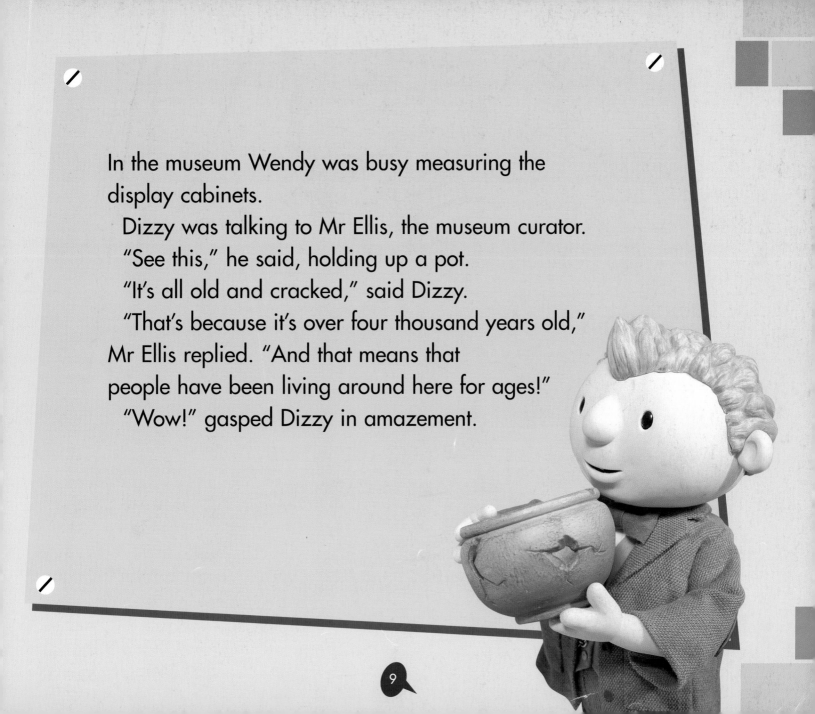

At Farmer Pickles's farm, Scoop was busy digging a deep trench when Bob spotted something.

"Hang on, Scoop!" called Bob as he bent down and brushed away some dirt.

"Look, a whopping big bone!" he said. "Ooh! Maybe it's a dinosaur bone!"

"Wow!" cried Scoop.

"Woahh!" Lofty said, shaking.

"And look – there's more than one!" said Bob excitedly. "I'm going to ring the museum and get an expert to come and have a look."

Mr Ellis rushed over to the field as soon as he heard the news. He carefully examined all the bones in the trench and smiled with delight.

"Scoop," he cried, "you've dug up a stegosaurus!"

Lofty looked puzzled. "A stega-what?"

"A stegosaurus – it's a sort of dinosaur," Scoop explained.

Bob and Mr Ellis collected all the bones together. "This is fantastic!" said Mr Ellis. "I think we've got a complete dinosaur skeleton!"

"These bones are very old and fragile," said Mr Ellis. "We'll need a special machine to take them to the museum."

"Oh..." said Scoop in a disappointed voice. He wanted to help carry the bones.

Then Mr Ellis added quickly, "But Scoop, I've got a very important job for you. Could you guard the bones while I'm gone?"

"You can count on me, Mr Ellis," said Scoop, with a big smile.

Bob covered the bones with a tarpaulin and followed Mr Ellis to the museum.

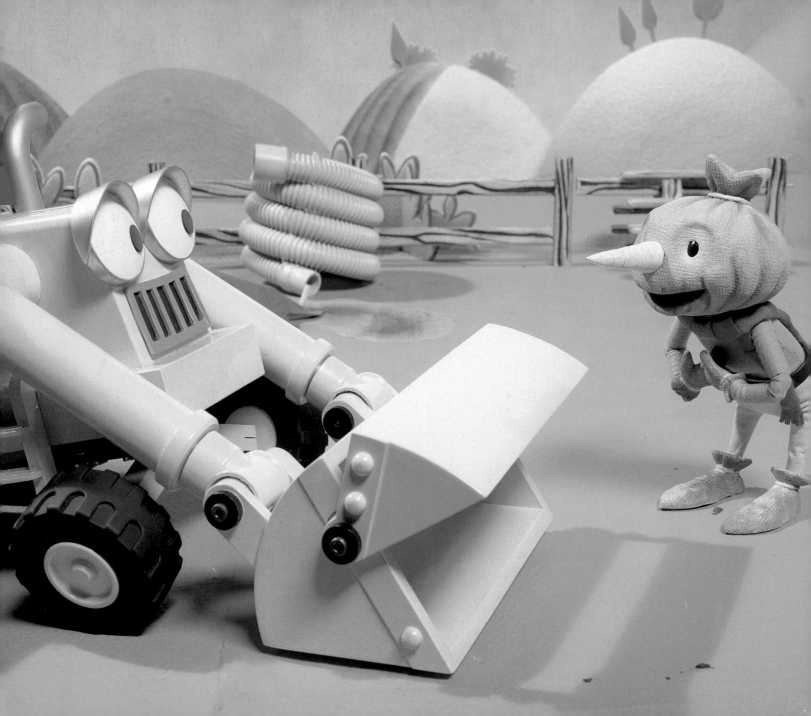

"Oooh, what's under there, Scoop?" asked Spud poking at the tarpaulin.

"I've just dug up some very important dinosaur's bones and I'm guarding them. Nobody's allowed to see them," said Scoop firmly.

"I've found some bones, too," said Spud with a cheeky grin. "I'll let you see mine if you let me see yours."

"Oh, OK then," Scoop said and went over to the next field to take a quick look.

"Hee, hee, hee!" giggled Spud as he peeped at the dinosaur's bones. "Cor! I'll borrow some of these!"

When the bones were delivered to the museum Mr Ellis studied the plan he'd made.

"That's strange," he said to Bob. "There are bits missing. If we had the complete stegosaurus skeleton, our little museum would have been famous all over the world."

"What a shame," said Bob. "Maybe there are still some bones left in the field. Let's go and have a look."

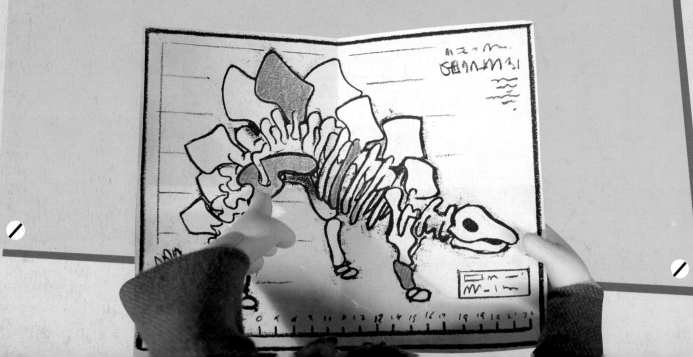

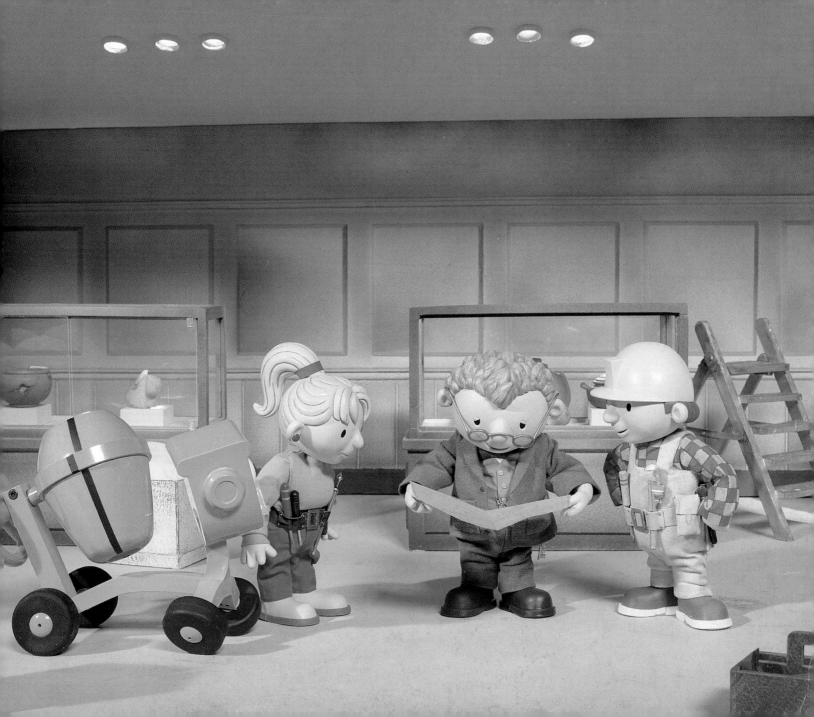

When they got back to the field the trench was empty.

"Maybe the missing bones are the ones Spud found?" said Scoop thoughtfully.

"**Spud?**" gasped Bob.

"Yes, Spud told me he'd found some bones in the next field, but I couldn't find them."

"You didn't leave our bones unguarded did you, Scoop?" Bob asked anxiously.

"Err… only for a few minutes," said Scoop. "Sorry, Bob."

"Oh, no! I think I know who's got our missing bones!" said Bob as he hurried off.

Meanwhile Spud was having a wonderful time with the stegosaurus bones.

"Roll up! Roll up! Come and see **SPUDULOSAURUS**, the scariest dinosaur ever!" he called proudly to Travis.

"It looks like a lot of old bones to me!" muttered Travis.

Then Bob turned up and Spud went unusually quiet.

"You found those bones under my tarpaulin sheet, didn't you, Spud?" said Bob.

"Er… yes. Sorry, Bob," muttered Spud.

"Spud, they're not yours!" said Bob sternly. "They're going to the museum where they belong!"

Mr Ellis fixed all the dinosaur bones into place.
"This is magnificent!" he said proudly. "A complete
stegosaurus skeleton!"
"Who would have thought that dinosaurs used
to live around here?" gasped Wendy.
"I'm **so** glad they don't now," giggled Dizzy.
"I wouldn't like to be chased by one of them!"
Mr Ellis gave Bob and Wendy a present
for Scoop.
"**Ooh!** What is it?" cried Dizzy.
"You'll see," smiled Mr Ellis.

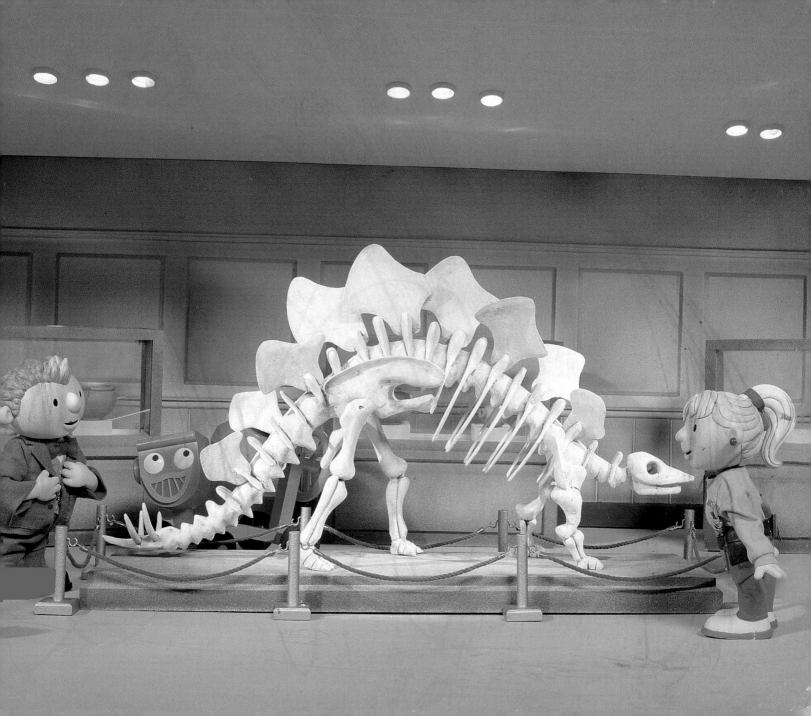

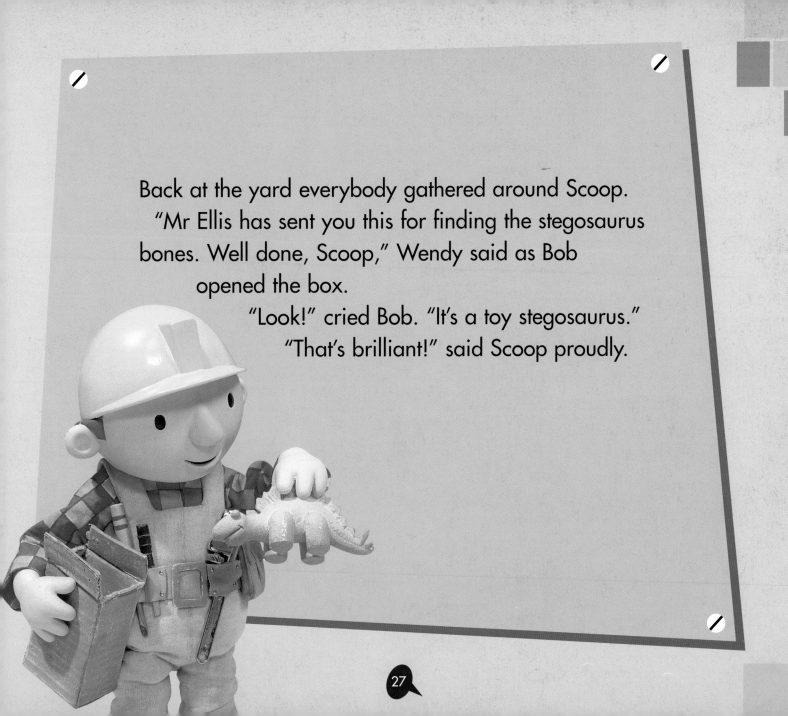

Back at the yard everybody gathered around Scoop. "Mr Ellis has sent you this for finding the stegosaurus bones. Well done, Scoop," Wendy said as Bob opened the box.

"Look!" cried Bob. "It's a toy stegosaurus."
"That's brilliant!" said Scoop proudly.

Suddenly the stegosaurus slipped out of Bob's fingers, flew into the air, and landed right on Pilchard's nose!

"**Wrreeeoowww!**" she howled and darted across the yard.

"If Pilchard's frightened of that, just think what she'd be like if she met a **Dizzyosaurus!**" giggled Dizzy. "**Raarghhh!**" she shouted as she roared like a dinosaur and rushed around the yard.

Scoop chuckled and rumbled after her, "Hee, hee! Yeah, and I'm a **Scooplodicus! Grrr, grrr!**"

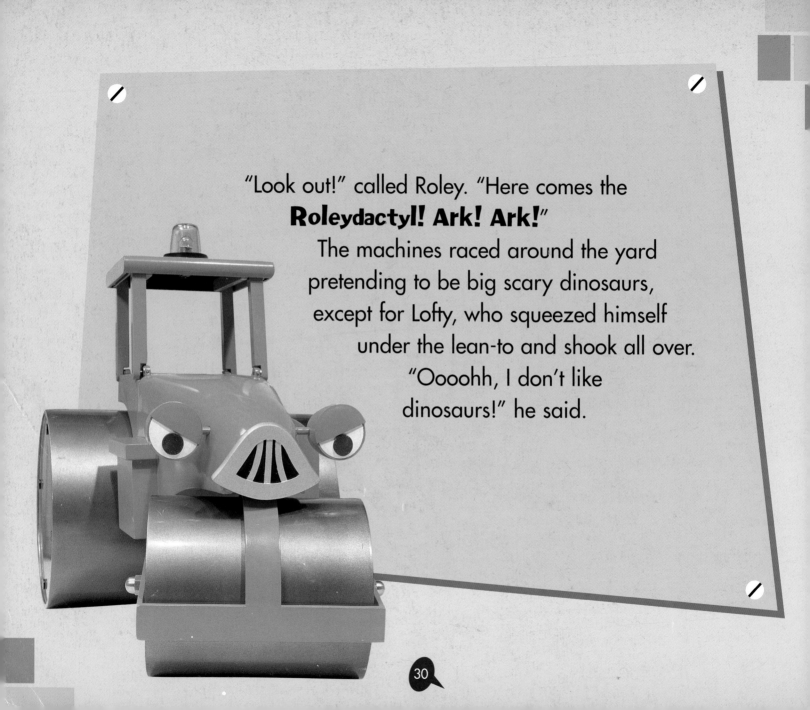

"Look out!" called Roley. "Here comes the **Roleydactyl! Ark! Ark!**" The machines raced around the yard pretending to be big scary dinosaurs, except for Lofty, who squeezed himself under the lean-to and shook all over. "Oooohh, I don't like dinosaurs!" he said.